Children Make Terrible Pets

Peter Brown

LB

Little, Brown and Company

New York Boston

When her secret admirer scurried into the open, Lucy could not believe her eyes.

So Lucy brought the critter home to show her mom.

Lucy and Squeaker were inseparable.

They played together.

They ate together.

They napped together.

Lucy and Squeaker did *everything* together. But it wasn't all fun and games.

He was impossible to potty train.

He ruined the furniture.

He caused problems wherever he went.

And just when Lucy thought things couldn't get any worse...

Lucy checked the usual hiding spots, but her pet was nowhere to be found.

Lucy had almost given up hope, when her sensitive nose caught a whiff of her Squeaker!

Lucy followed Squeaker's scent this way and that, across the entire forest until finally...

...she found Squeaker!

But something had changed.

Squeaker didn't seem like a pet anymore.

Lucy knew what she had to do.

Good-bye, Squeaker.

Lucy had a lot to think about on her walk home.

The End

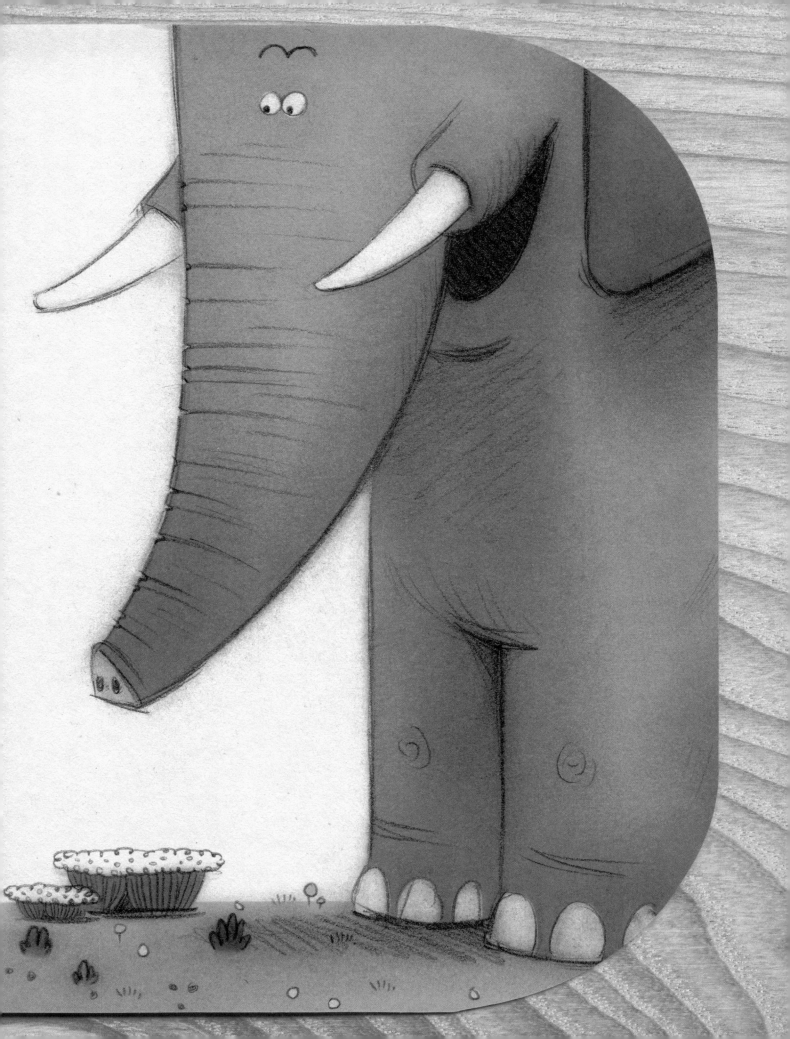

For Ella and Owen (my niece and nephew)
—P.B.

Little, Brown and Company • Hachette Book Group • 237 Park Avenue, New York, NY 10017 Visit our website at www.lb-kids.com • Little, Brown and Company is a division of Hachette Book Group, Inc. • The Little, Brown name and logo are trademarks of Hachette Book Group, Inc.

First Edition: September 2010 • 10 9 8 7 6 5 4 3 2 1 • SC • Printed in China

Brown, Peter, 1979—
  Children make terrible pets / by Peter Brown. — 1st ed.
    p. cm.
  Summary: When Lucy, a young bear, discovers a boy lost in the woods, she asks her mother if she can have him as a pet, only to find him impossible to train.
  ISBN 978-0-316-01548-6
  [1. Pets—Fiction. 2. Bears—Fiction. 3. Lost children—Fiction. 4. Humorous stories.] I. Title.
  PZ7.B81668Ch 2010
  [E]—dc22   2010004982

The illustrations for this book were rendered in pencil on paper, with cut construction paper and wood and a wee bit of digital tweaking. The narration text was set in Clarendon, and the word balloons were handlettered by the author.

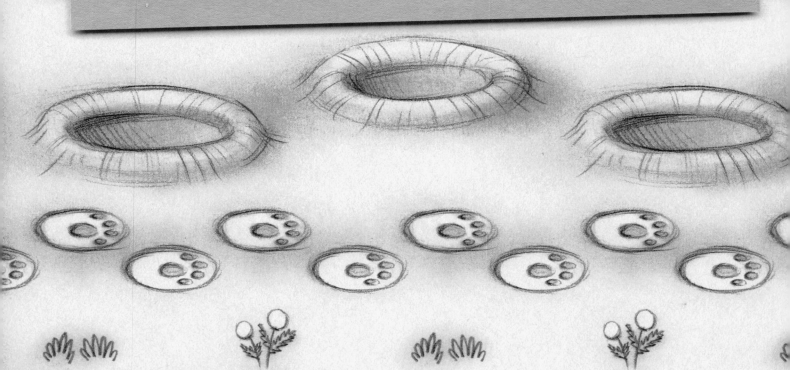